That
New River Train

Pictured by Lucy Hawkinson

ALBERT WHITMAN & Company   Chicago

Books by Lucy Hawkinson

Dance, Dance, Amy–Chan!
Days I Like

Adapted from *More Songs to Grow On* by Beatrice Landeck
Copyright Edward B. Marks Music Corporation
Used by Permission

Standard Book Number 8075–7823–1
Library of Congress Card Number 76–126438
Illustrations © 1970 by Lucy Hawkinson
Published simultaneously in Canada by George J. McLeod, Limited, Toronto
Lithographed in the United States of America

That New River Train

I'm riding on that new river train,
I'm riding on that new river train—
Same old train that brought me here,
Going to carry me home again.

Jenny, you can't love one,
Jenny, you can't love one—
You can't love one and still have fun,
Jenny, you can't love one.

one **1**

Jenny, you can't love two,
Jenny, you can't love two—
You can't love two, I tell you true,
Jenny, you can't love two.

two 2

Jenny, you can't love three,
Jenny, you can't love three—
You can't love three and sing with me,
Jenny, you can't love three.

three **3**

Jenny, you can't love four,
Jenny, you can't love four—
You can't love four and squeeze in my door,
Jenny, you can't love four.

four 4

Jenny, you can't love five,
Jenny, you can't love five—
You can't love five and go for a drive,
Jenny, you can't love five.

five 5

Jenny, you can't love six,
Jenny, you can't love six—
You can't love six and teach them all tricks,
Jenny, you can't love six.

six **6**

Jenny, you can't love seven,
Jenny, you can't love seven—
You can't love seven and get into heaven,
Jenny, you can't love seven.

seven 7

Jenny, you can't love eight,
Jenny, you can't love eight—
You can't love eight and keep them straight,
Jenny, you can't love eight.

eight **8**

Jenny, you can't love nine,
Jenny, you can't love nine—
You can't love nine and march in a line,
Jenny, you can't love nine.

nine 9

Jenny, you can't love ten,
Jenny, you can't love ten—
You can't love ten and sing this song again,
Jenny, you can't love ten.

ten **10**

Jenny, you must love all,
Jenny, you must love all—
You must love all, both big and small,
Jenny, you must love all.

ALL

I'm riding on that new river train,
I'm riding on that new river train—
Same old train that brought me here,
Going to carry me home again.

That New River Train

I'm   rid-ing on that   new   riv-er

train, I'm   rid-ing on that new   riv-er   train—

Same   old   train   that   brought   me   here,   Going to

car-ry   me   home   a - gain.

Verses

1 Jenny, you can't love one,
 Jenny, you can't love one—
 You can't love one and still have fun,
 Jenny, you can't love one.

2 Jenny, you can't love two . . .
 You can't love two, I tell you true . . .

3 Jenny, you can't love three . . .
 You can't love three and sing with me . . .

4 Jenny, you can't love four . . .
 You can't love four and squeeze in my door . . .

5 Jenny, you can't love five . . .
 You can't love five and go for a drive . . .

6 Jenny, you can't love six . . .
 You can't love six and teach them all tricks . . .

7 Jenny, you can't love seven . . .
 You can't love seven and get into heaven . . .

8 Jenny, you can't love eight . . .
 You can't love eight and keep them straight . . .

9 Jenny, you can't love nine . . .
 You can't love nine and march in a line . . .

10 Jenny, you can't love ten . . .
 You can't love ten and sing this song again . . .

11 Jenny, you must love all . . .
 You must love all, both big and small . . .

Adapted from "More Songs to Grow On" by Beatrice Landeck

About the Artist

Lucy Ozone Hawkinson was born in California. Her parents had emigrated there from Japan, where her mother had been a kindergarten teacher. Her father was a businessman.

World War II interrupted life in the West. After a period at an internment camp, the Ozones moved to Chicago. For a time, Lucy worked for the Relocation Authority in Washington, D.C., but when she rejoined her family, she took classes at the Chicago Academy of Fine Arts. She worked on mechanical illustrations, gradually moving toward more creative illustration and freelance assignments.

Lucy is the wife of artist and author John Hawkinson. Their daughters, Anne and Julia, inspired their mother's picture book, *Dance, Dance, Amy-Chan!* which describes an annual Buddhist festival in Chicago.

Mr. and Mrs. Hawkinson have collaborated on illustrations, but each has produced work independently. *That New River Train* grew out of Lucy Hawkinson's pleasure in singing folksongs to guitar accompaniment for her daughters and their friends.